BERLIOZ
THE BEAR

written and illustrated by
Jan Brett

PAPERSTAR

Penguin Young Readers Group

To Joe

Typography by David Gatti. Airbrush backgrounds by Joseph Hearne.
Library of Congress Cataloging-in-Publication Data
Brett, Jan.   Berlioz the bear/written and illustrated by Jan Brett.   p.   cm.
Summary: Berlioz the bear and his fellow musicians are due to play for the town ball
when their bandwagon becomes stuck in a hole in the road. A strange buzzing in Berlioz's
double bass turns into a surprise that saves the day.   [1. Bear—Fiction. 2. Animals—Fiction.
3. Musicians—Fiction.]   I. Title. PZ7.B7559Be   1991   [E]—dc20   90-37634   CIP   AC
ISBN 978-0-698-11399-2
25 27 29 30 28 26

Zum. Zum buzzz. Zum. Zum. Buzz. Berlioz had been practicing for
weeks, and now just when the orchestra was going to play in the village
square for a gala ball, a strange buzz was coming from his double bass.
  "Why now?" Berlioz said to himself.

The musicians arrived with their instruments. As Berlioz
watched them climb aboard the bandwagon, all he could think
about was his buzzing bass. What if his bass buzzed during the ball?
What if the dancers stopped dancing and laughed at him?

Zum, zum, buzz. Zum, zum, buzz, he imagined.

Berlioz picked up the reins and clucked to the mule. Off they
went down the road. He was so worried that he didn't see a hole
in the road ahead. Suddenly, the wagon lurched to a stop. The
front wheel was stuck in the hole. The mule took one look back,
sat down and yawned.

"Oh dear," said Berlioz, as he tried to get the mule to stand up and pull the bandwagon out of the hole. "What can we do? We'll be late for the ball."

"I'll help you," said a rooster who was passing by on his way to the ball. "I'll just tug on the rope and pull you out," he bragged. The rooster pulled and pulled, but the mule stayed put.

A tabby who had been watching from the top of a fence spoke up smugly.

"That isn't a job for a featherweight," he purred. "I'll do it for you."

And he took hold of the rope and pulled. But the mule wouldn't move.

"Oh my," said Berlioz. "At this rate we'll never get to the ball on time.

Everyone put on your concert tailcoats so we'll be ready to start as soon as we get there."

The

Just then a schnauzer came trotting over the hill.

He took one look at the cat and sniffed. "A fur ball like you can't pull a bandwagon. Here, let me have that rope."

He panted and pulled, but the wagon stayed in the hole.

Berlioz handed out the music.

"Everyone take out your instruments. We'll start tuning up here."

Along came a prancing billy goat.

He looked at the schnauzer and snorted. "Move over, squirt, and let me do it. I'll have this wagon out in no time."

The billy goat strained forward, but to his surprise he got nowhere.

Berlioz checked his pocket watch There wasn't much time
left. He was about to give up when he heard a new voice.
    "Allow me," said a plow horse coming across the field.
"This will be easy. I spend my days pulling."
    But even the plow horse couldn't move the mule.

Berlioz tugged at his ears. It was almost time for the ball to begin.
He looked around and saw a large ox lumbering toward them.

"Everyone tune up. Here comes someone who can pull us out!"

"You're saved!" roared the ox. "This poor plow horse means well,
but only I am strong enough to pull a bandwagon full of musicians."

He twisted the rope around his horns and gave a mighty tug.
The animals held their breaths. But the mule wouldn't budge.
The clock on the tower started to chime eight o'clock.

"Oh no," Berlioz shouted. In desperation he pulled his bow across the strings and to his dismay he heard *Zum…zum…buzz…buzzzz.* All the musicians turned to look at the buzzing double bass.

Out of the bass shot a very angry bee. It had been disturbed once too often. The first thing it saw as it flew out of the bass was the hindquarters of the mule.

Buzzzzz

With one giant sting, the bee made the mule jump to his feet and pull the bandwagon of musicians out of the hole, down the road and into the village square before the bells had stopped chiming.

The audience roared. "What an entrance!" they cried, and the orchestra, already dressed and tuned, began to play.

Zum, zum, zum,

Zum, zum, zum.

It was hard to say who had more fun at the ball, the musicians or the dancers. Berlioz had never played better.

"Encore, Berlioz! Encore!"
Berlioz came forward.
"Thank you all. And this evening, I would like to dedicate
our encore to the buzzing bee."